BAINTE DEN STOC

WITHDRAWN FROM
DÚN LAOGHAIRE-RATHDOWN COUNTY
LIBRARY STOCK

D0119721

and what would we do
without Mister Newman?

Copyright © 1999 by Gus Clarke

The rights of Gus Clarke to be identified as the author and illustrator of this work have
been asserted by him in accordance with the Copyright, Designs and Patents Act, 1988.

First published in Great Britain in 1999 by Andersen Press Ltd.,
20 Vauxhall Bridge Road, London SW1V 2SA. Published in Australia by Random House Australia Pty.,
20 Alfred Street, Milsons Point, Sydney, NSW 2061. All rights reserved. Colour separated in Italy by
Fotoriproduzione Grafiche, Verona. Printed and bound in Italy by Grafiche AZ, Verona.

10   9   8   7   6   5   4   3   2   1

British Library Cataloguing in Publication Data available.

ISBN 0 86264 884 X

This book has been printed on acid-free paper

What would we do without Missus Mac?

GUS CLARKE

Andersen Press · London

What would we do without Missus Mac?
She's always around when you need a hand;

when things get stuck

or they won't stay up.

She's always there when you need her most;

to put things together

or keep them apart.

Where would we *be* without Missus Mac?
Liam would never have learned how to swim

or Ryan to read

or Samantha to skip.

Felicity wouldn't have gone very far

and Paul just wouldn't be with us at all.

Where would we *go* without Missus Mac?
She gets us there safely

and brings us all back.

We've been to see old things

and new ones.

We've been to run races

and we *all* won.

And now she's leaving! We're all here to say goodbye.
But what will we *do* without Missus Mac?

What can we say? There's only one thing...

MISSUS MAC, PLEASE DON'T GO!

And what do you think she said?

"Okay. I'll stay…Well, what would I do without *you!*"